BOOK NEWS

Sign up for exclusive updates and offers at
news.jljarvis.com

GET THE AUDIOBOOK

jljarvis.com/kir

A KISS IN THE RAIN

A KISS IN THE RAIN

A CONTEMPORARY ROMANCE NOVELETTE SET IN IRELAND

J.L. JARVIS

BOOKBINDER PRESS

A KISS IN THE RAIN

ISBN (ebook) 978-1-942767-81-7

ISBN (paperback) 978-1-942767-82-4

Published by Bookbinder Press

bookbinderpress.com

A KISS IN THE RAIN

"And that's why I'll never get married," Grace Luong said into her phone as she watched rain streak down the window of O'Brien's B&B in Ballykilduff. Beyond the rain-blurred glass, the spire of the village church rose against steel-gray clouds.

Her assistant leaned into the phone lens. "That's a little dramatic. Couples call off weddings. It happens."

"Not like this."

"Why?" Megan asked, looking understandably curious but not shocked. In five years, they'd seen couples fail to make it those last several steps to the altar, but this was a first.

"Oh, Megan." She looked at Megan's confused face on the phone screen. "A fortune-teller told her she and the groom were siblings in a past life."

"No!" Megan looked pained as she tried not to laugh.

Grace nodded. "So, she canceled the wedding."

"Sorry for laughing, but really?"

"During her bachelorette party, they passed a neon sign in a window and pulled over." Grace pinched the bridge of her nose. "Two years of planning—not to mention their future together—all flushed away. And don't even get me started on how we had to schedule everything around Lughnasadh."

"Oh, right, that Celtic harvest festival."

"August first. Olivia had read online that it was the most spiritually auspicious day for new beginnings." Grace couldn't keep the sarcasm from her voice. "She wouldn't even consider another date. Do you know how hard it was coordinating vendors all across County Wicklow for her mystically perfect wedding on that particular day? Now I have musicians, florists, and caterers all booked for a date that was supposedly destined for perfection—except for the tiny detail that there won't be a wedding."

"Wow. Fortune-tellers *and* druids? She really went all in on the Irish mysticism thing."

"And now she can't look at James without feeling weird."

"Wow."

"Yeah. And I'm not being dramatic. I'm being practical. I spend my life orchestrating other people's perfect moments, Meg. You know how many couples I've worked with? Two hundred and twelve."

Megan's eyes sparkled. "And now they're all disgustingly happy."

"Some are." Grace's voice softened. "The ones who look at each other like they've forgotten anyone else exists, who don't care if the flowers are perfect or the cake arrives on time because they're just...happy to be getting married." She traced a raindrop down the window with her finger. "You know how many times I've felt even a flutter of what they're feeling?"

"Grace..."

"Zero."

Megan did that sympathetic pouty mouth thing she did when she couldn't find a single word of encouragement. Her expression brightened. "But you're in Ireland!"

"Yes, to oversee the last-minute wedding arrangements at Clonmara House. I guess I can cross that off my calendar," Grace said.

"And write in 'take the week off!'"

"What?" The thought hadn't even occurred to Grace.

"Oh, come on! When's the last time you had a real vacation? And don't say Dave and Elise's destination wedding in Maui. You were working."

"Well, yeah. But it was Hawaii."

Megan nodded. "And it was two years ago. I just checked your calendar." Megan's voice softened. "Look, let me handle it. I'll contact the vendors. You're already in Ireland—enjoy it."

"I should at least—"

"Take the week off? Yes." Megan's no-nonsense nod tipped the scale.

"Are you sure?"

"Positive. Now go." She shooed Grace away with her free hand and then ended the call before Grace could reply.

"Well, I don't know about a week." Grace stood at the window. "But a few days would be nice." She couldn't deny that this corner of Wicklow had captured her heart. Maybe it was the way the village seemed to exist in its own pocket of time or how the sea mist rolled in over the cliffs like a dream. She opened her phone app and moved up her return flight. She loved Megan's idea, but a week was too long. She had a business to run. A few days would be perfect.

The sound of bells made her look up. The village church was spilling light and music onto the wet flagstones, adding to the charm of the quaint village. Without thinking, Grace grabbed her camera and rain jacket and headed outside.

"Going to see young Katie's wedding, are you?" Mrs. O'Brien called from behind the B&B's front desk. "Sure, and you won't see a prettier bride this year. But if you're wanting real romance, you should visit the old black church ruins up the hill. That's where the real stories are."

Grace paused, suspecting the innkeeper was laying it on pretty thick for a tourist, but curiosity got the better of her. "The black church?"

"Ah, that's what gives our little Ballykilduff its name. There's a tale about two lovers who—" Mrs.

O'Brien stopped as the front bell chimed. "Another time, dear. You'll want to hurry if you're going to see the bride."

"Oh, I'm not—" she began, but Mrs. O'Brien was already greeting another guest. Grace reached the churchyard just as the heavy wooden doors swung open.

The bride appeared first, radiant in a simple lace dress, then the groom. They paused at the top of the steps, oblivious to the light rain, lost in each other's eyes. Grace lifted her camera instinctively, then lowered it. Some moments weren't meant to be captured by strangers.

The couple ran down the steps through a shower of rose petals, laughing as their guests cheered in a mix of English and Irish. Grace pressed a hand to her throat, fighting an unexpected surge of emotion. It wasn't envy she felt. It was longing. Not for a wedding. She'd seen so many of those they barely registered a blip on her romantic radar. What struck her was the incandescent joy on the bride's face— that bone-deep certainty that she'd found that one perfect person to love and to cherish... Grace swallowed.

"You should see Clonmara House," a voice said beside her.

Grace turned to find the weathered taxi driver, Tommy, who'd driven her from the train station.

"Oh, I've seen it in pictures."

"I heard your wedding was canceled."

"Not mine. I just plan them." She was surprised he remembered their earlier conversation.

"Shame about that. It's a grand place, just the same." He broke off, studying the sky. "Speaking of shame, looks like we're in for a proper storm. Need a lift anywhere?"

Grace looked up at the darkening clouds, then down at her camera. "That depends on the weather. You know... On second thought, I would like to see Clonmara House—for my portfolio."

Tommy's eyes crinkled as he looked up at the sky. "I'd say you've got about two hours before the rain starts."

Grace was impressed. "Two hours? You can tell that by looking at the sky?"

His eyes twinkled as he lifted his phone. "No, I've got an app."

Grace smiled and glanced down, feeling foolish. "That should be plenty of time."

Tommy's taxi wound along the coastal road, and Clonmara House emerged from the mist like something from a dream—all weathered gray stone and tall windows catching the fleeting sunlight, perched above the sea as if it had grown straight from the cliffs themselves.

"Beautiful, isn't it?" Tommy said softly. "Been in the Callahan family for hundreds of years. Young Sean Callahan's many times great grandmother is quite a story herself." He pulled up to the public beach access. "Two hours? Would you like me to come back then?"

"No, that's okay. I'll call you."

"You'll get your best signal up by the house."

Grace thanked him and got out of the taxi. As she headed for the beach, Tommy called out from the window. "Mind you, stay on the public paths. And watch the weather—storms come up quick along this coast."

With a smile and a wave, she was off. She drew in a deep breath, and the salt-tinged air revived her from her jet lag. The morning sun cast its light on the ancient stones, making the house seem to glow against the moody storm clouds. She took a few snaps and followed the public path that wound along the cliff's edge, stopping every few yards to capture another angle. The property was even more stunning up close with gardens that somehow managed to look both manicured and wild, stone walls softened by climbing roses, and everywhere the dramatic back-drop of the Irish Sea.

She was so absorbed in photographing a massive oak tree that she didn't hear approaching footsteps until a deep bark made her jump. Grace spun around to find herself face-to-face with an enormous shaggy dog, its tail wagging as it looked up hopefully at her with gentle eyes.

"Finn! Here!"

The dog's owner appeared around the corner of

the path—tall, dark-haired, with striking green eyes and an expression that suggested he wasn't nearly as friendly as his pet. In his worn jeans and a navy sweater that had seen better days, he looked every bit the estate groundskeeper.

"I'm sorry," Grace said quickly. "I know I'm technically on private property, but I was just photographing—"

"The public path ends at the stone marker," he said, his accent a pleasant lilt despite his stern tone. "You're about twenty feet past it."

"Oh! I didn't realize." Grace took a step back, but the huge dog—Finn—followed, nudging her hand for attention. Despite his size, there was something endearingly gentle about him. "He's beautiful. What breed is he?"

Something in the man's face softened slightly. "Irish Wolfhound. Apparently, he's forgotten all his dignified breeding." This last was directed at the dog, who had flopped onto his back, clearly expecting a belly rub.

Grace couldn't help laughing as she obliged. As she stood, she extended her hand. "I'm Grace Luong. I was actually supposed to be handling an event here next week. I'm a wedding planner. But..." she trailed off, not wanting to get into the past-life sibling saga.

"Ah. The canceled wedding." He studied her for a moment. "If the wedding is canceled, then why are you here?"

"For future reference," she said quickly. "I do a lot of destination weddings, and this property is..." She gestured at the stunning vista behind him. "Well, it's perfect."

He looked like he was about to say something else, but a distant rumble of thunder interrupted him. They both looked up at clouds that had grown dramatically darker in the last few minutes.

"You should head back," he said with a nod toward the public path.

Grace nodded and leaned down. "Nice to meet you, Finn."

The dog woofed softly, and as she straightened, she could have sworn his owner's mouth twitched toward a smile. "You, too..." She realized he'd never told her his name.

"Sean."

Even as he said it, he seemed reluctant to do so. She wouldn't say he was rude, but she wouldn't call him warm and friendly, either. She supposed people skills weren't at the top of a groundskeeper's job requirements.

As they parted ways, the light kept shifting, creating new shadows and new possibilities. She'd just discovered a weathered stone archway half-hidden by climbing roses when the first drops of rain began to fall.

"Not yet," she muttered, adjusting her camera settings. The rain made everything glisten, and the moody sky created a dramatic backdrop that was absolutely perfect.

A crack of thunder made her jump, prompting her to call for a taxi. When she checked her phone, her heart sank. No signal. Tommy had said she'd get her best signal up by the house, so she headed that way.

The rain intensified suddenly, turning from a scenic backdrop to a genuine problem in seconds. Tucking her camera into her backpack, she hurried toward the house. The path forked, then forked again until she didn't know anymore where the public path was. Beneath the dark clouds, all she could see was the house on the hill, so she headed that way, checking her phone all the while for a signal.

Another thunder cracked, closer this time. Through the curtain of rain, she kept her eyes on Clonmara House's lights. The rain was coming sideways now, soaking through her thin jacket.

Still no signal. "Great," she said aloud. "Time to swallow my pride."

Up close, the front door of Clonmara House was impossibly grand—tall, dark wood with iron fittings. Grace hesitated as water dripped from her forehead and nose, then reached for the brass knocker.

Before she could grasp it, the door swung open. Sean stood there, without his wolfhound this time, with an expression somewhere between annoyance and amusement.

"I'm so sorry to intrude," Grace began, water

dripping from her hair, "but I can't get a signal. I was wondering if I could possibly use your phone to call a taxi. If you wouldn't mind asking the owner—"

"I'm the owner," he said, his mouth twitching slightly.

Grace felt the heat rise in her cheeks despite her rain-chilled skin. "Oh! I'm so sorry, I thought you were..." She continued under her breath, "Not the owner."

A booming bark interrupted her as Finn appeared behind his owner, tail wagging in delighted recognition. With a sideways glance at his dog, Sean said, "Come in."

The entrance hall made her wedding planner's heart skip a beat. A marble-tiled floor led to a sweeping staircase. Was that a suit of armor in the corner? She was trying not to drip onto what looked like a priceless Oriental rug when an elderly woman appeared with a stack of towels.

"Oh, you poor thing! You're soaked through. Sean, don't just stand there—take her into the study to warm up by the fire." She handed Grace the towels. "I'm Mrs. Flynn, the housekeeper. And I see you've already met Mr. Callahan."

"Yes," Grace managed, still mortified. "We met earlier. When I was trespassing."

That got an actual smile from him, brief but transformative. "The study is this way. Mrs. Flynn, could you—"

"Bring some tea?" the housekeeper said, smiling.

"And maybe a drop of medicinal whiskey to ward off any chill."

The study turned out to be the modern glass-walled addition Grace had admired from the outside. But now, with rain lashing the windows and a fire crackling in a surprisingly traditional fireplace, it felt less like a statement of contemporary architecture and more like a ship's bridge in a storm. Comfortable leather chairs were arranged near the fire, and books lined the two walls that weren't glass.

"I'm really sorry about this," Grace said, sinking into one of the chairs. Finn immediately flopped at her feet. "Both for trespassing earlier and…" She sighed and gestured toward herself. "This."

"I'm surprised Tommy didn't warn you."

"About you?"

Sean's eyes lit with amusement. "No, about the signal—and the weather. It's been threatening rain all day."

"Yeah, come to think of it, he did mention both. Sorry."

"Let's call it even," Sean said, settling into the opposite chair. "I could have mentioned I was the owner when we met on the path."

"Why didn't you?"

He studied her for a moment. "People tend to act differently when they know who I am."

"The curse of being the eligible lord of the manor?" The words slipped out before Grace could stop them. "I mean—sorry—occupational hazard. I've planned a few too many Jane Austen-themed weddings."

To her relief, he laughed. "Not exactly."

"Cursed or eligible?" She'd meant it as a joke but found herself curious to know the answer.

Sean raised an eyebrow. "Hopefully, just the latter. Although there are a few local matchmakers who'd love to amend that, but finding someone who'd have me proved too much of a challenge."

"I doubt that." Grace smiled, but she was serious. Barring some hideous character flaws, this was not the sort of guy women said no to unless they had an aversion to tall, broad-shouldered men with striking green eyes a girl could get lost in and a shock of nearly black hair. Grace's thoughts strayed as she imagined combing her fingers into that hair.

"It's the legend—the same thing that draws people like you."

"Sorry?" Her thoughts had clearly gone off on a tangent, and now she was totally lost. "People like me?"

Seeming to mistake her confusion for offense, he explained, "Wedding people. The venue, the legend —it puts matchmaking on people's minds."

Grace supposed that was fair enough. "Wait, what legend?" She should have known about that. But the venue had been her client's choice, so she hadn't made a historical study of Ballykilduff. She'd just made the arrangements.

"Ballykilduff—the Black Church." His eyes twinkled. "Some say you can find true love there. I'll leave that to you to decide."

"I'm intrigued." That was no lie. Everything about this place and its owner intrigued her.

"There's a story, but I'm not the one to tell it. I'm more of a tech guy than a poet."

Grace glanced around at the Georgian study and outside, where wild waves crashed against the rocky shore as rain came down in sheets. "Tech isn't the first thought that comes to mind when I look around here."

"Exactly."

She waited for him to elaborate, but nothing followed. "Exactly?"

"I recently moved back home."

"Oh?" Grace realized she was working awfully hard to learn more about him, but she couldn't help herself.

"I used to have an office in Dublin, and now, I'm here."

She sensed an unvoiced *end of story*.

Mrs. Flynn returned with a tray of tea, a decanter of whiskey, and an impressive, tiered stand of finger sandwiches and cakes. "Tommy's on his way in the taxi. I'll let you know when he's arrived."

"Thank you, Mrs. Flynn. This looks amazing!"

The older woman thanked her, cast a knowing look at Sean, and left.

When they were both situated with beverages and something to eat, Grace said, "So... this legend."

"You'll have to get the full story from someone else. Like I said, I'm not a storyteller. It's one of those star-crossed lovers' tales that romantic sorts like. Our culture is full of them." He shrugged it off and took a sip of whiskey.

"I get that. All that romance can get—"

"Annoying?" He grinned.

"To be honest? Yes, now and then. I mean... I love my work—planning weddings. I make people happy, right?"

He offered a hesitant nod.

"But when it comes to love, people go kind of nuts." She rolled her eyes. "It's not black magic. Not to knock your black church—which I'm sure is enchanting—but this is real life."

He looked puzzled, so she went on. "I mean, who calls off a wedding because a fortune teller told you that in a past life, your groom was your brother?"

Sean's eyebrows rose. "Is that what happened with your wedding? The one that was supposed to be here?" He didn't even try to suppress his amusement.

Grace winced and nodded. "Like I said, when it comes to love, some people will believe anything."

Something flickered in Sean's eyes, but before he could respond, Mrs. Flynn returned. "Dear, your taxi's arrived."

AN HOUR LATER, Grace sat cross-legged on her bed at the B&B with her hair wrapped in a towel and a laptop balanced on her knees. The hot bath had helped with the chill from the rain, but she still felt unsettled. She told herself she was just looking up Clonmara House to learn about its history—purely professional research. But her fingers typed *Sean Callahan Ireland* instead.

"Oh." The word escaped in a small breath as she stared at her screen.

The first result was a Forbes profile, "Irish Tech Prodigy Sean Callahan Sells Startup for €850M." *Wow, the camera loves you!* The photo showed him in a perfectly tailored suit at a tech conference, looking every inch the successful CEO. But it was the casual confidence in his stance that caught her eye—the same quiet self-possession she'd noticed even when she'd thought he was a groundskeeper.

She clicked through two more articles. Sean had built his fintech company from scratch, developing a revolutionary payment processing system that trans-formed how small businesses handled international transactions. The tech press called him brilliant but enigmatic, especially after he stepped away from Dublin's Silicon Docks at the height of his success.

"Callahan surprised industry insiders," one article read, "by declining several high-profile CEO positions to return to his family's historic Wicklow estate."

Grace closed her laptop and flopped back against

the pillows. No wonder he hadn't corrected her assumption about who he was. She'd treated him like...well, like a normal person. And based on these articles, that probably didn't happen often.

Still feeling unsettled, she dried her hair and headed downstairs. She was hungry, and Mrs. O'Brien had mentioned that the Harbor Light pub served decent pub grub.

The Harbor Light was everything Grace had hoped for. It was all warm wood panels, a glowing hearth, and old black-and-white photos of the village lining the walls. Above the bar, a massive brass ship's lantern cast a gentle glow, its weathered patina suggesting it had once guided sailors through storms far darker than the one brewing outside. Soft music wove through the gentle buzz of conversation as Grace found a small table near the fireplace and ordered beef stew and a pint of Guinness. The warmth slowly seeped into her bones, chasing away the last of the afternoon's chill.

A burst of laughter drew her attention to the bar, where a white-haired woman was holding court among a group of what she assumed to be tourists. Her face was lined with years of smiles, and she had the sort of twinkling eyes that suggested she knew all the best stories.

"You want to know about the black church, do

you?" The white-haired woman gestured to the old photographs on the wall. "Look, there it is, but centuries ago, its stones glistened like morning frost. But that was before the night love was lost, back when Clonmara House was new."

Grace found herself turning in her chair to listen.

"There was a girl there—she must have been about your age, dear." The woman nodded to one of the tourists. "From Clonmara House itself—one of the first Callahan brides. Kathleen was her name, and she had hair as dark as midwinter midnight and eyes that changed like the sea—one moment calm as summer dawn, the next stormy as a November gale."

The storyteller's eyes grew distant. "Her father had arranged a fine match for her—a very suitable lad for a proper landowner's daughter. But hearts pay no heed to what's proper, do they? No, Kathleen's heart belonged to Rory Sullivan, a merchant's son with clever hands and a smile that could chase the storm clouds from the blackest sky—except for one fateful night."

Grace set down her glass, caught by the ache in the woman's voice.

"Too desperately in love to be parted, they made their plans in whispers. On the night before she was to be wed, they would meet at the church when the moon was at its highest. But, oh, the storm that came in from the sea that night! It was the kind that makes the very cliffs shudder and sends the waves crashing into the rocks like banshees keening."

The pub had grown quieter as more people turned to listen.

"Down the treacherous path our Kathleen came, her cloak pulled tight against the wind. In the church, she lit a candle and set it in the window as a beacon to guide her love there." The woman's voice dropped lower. "But on the cliff path, where the rocks were slick with rain and as treacherous as a serpent's back, Rory's horse lost its footing."

Someone gasped softly.

"The fall didn't kill him, thanks be to God, but it left him badly hurt and unable to move. There he lay on that cruel path, able to see her candle flickering in the church window, yet too far to reach it. They say he called out to her, but sure, what chance did a mortal voice have against such a howling wind?"

The storyteller paused to sip her drink, but her eyes were far away. "In the church, Kathleen waited long through the night as her candle burned lower and lower. With each flicker of the flame, her heart broke a bit more. When morning came, her father found her half-frozen, still watching the door. Believing her love had abandoned her, she walked down the aisle that very day with the man her father had chosen."

"But what happened to Rory?" someone whispered.

"By the time they found him, she was married.

That very night, as the wedding feast began, the storm returned with a vengeance like no one had ever seen. It was on that night that lightning struck the church and turned it black. They say it was Heaven's own tears crystallized in the stone to mark a true love lost."

Grace realized she was holding her breath.

"But here's the thing about true love." The woman leaned forward, her voice dropping to a whisper that somehow carried through the hushed pub. "A love that strong leaves echoes in a place, like an old tin whistle tune in the air. The legend promises that lovers who brave a storm to reach the black church will always find their way back to each other."

"And did they?" Grace found herself asking. "Did Kathleen and Rory ever find each other again?"

The storyteller's eyes twinkled. "Ah, now that's another tale entirely—one best saved for another night when the wind's not so wild and we've time to do it justice." She glanced toward the door. "Though if you're wanting to know more about the Callahans and their storms, you might ask young Sean there himself."

Grace turned just as the pub door flew open with a gust of wind that set the candles flickering. Rain misted in, carrying the scent of the sea. And there in the doorway stood Sean, the storm at his back making his tall frame look like something out of a legend himself.

Their eyes met across the pub while the story-teller's words still hung in the air, and for a moment, Grace could have sworn time itself held its breath.

Then Sean nodded slightly and turned to the bar. When he left a few minutes later, the wind caught at him again, and this time, when he glanced back, their eyes held for a heartbeat longer than necessary.

The storyteller watched this small drama play out with knowing eyes. When the door closed behind Sean, she smiled into her glass and murmured, "Some stories, you see, are still being written."

Grace turned back to her dinner and tried to ignore her racing heart. It was only the warmth of the fire, the ale, and a well-told tale.

But later that night, she dreamed of candlelight in windows, lovers lost in storms, and of green eyes that watched her across an old Irish tavern.

THE MORNING AIR had that freshly washed feeling that followed a storm. Grace adjusted her camera strap and consulted her phone's map again, though the signal kept wavering. The Black Church ruins were visible on a distant hill, stark against a brilliant blue sky, but the path there was less obvious than she'd hoped.

She'd already wandered down three wrong lanes and photographed countless sheep. The last one had given her such a judgmental look that she'd actually apologized to it.

The rumble of an engine made her turn. A vintage Land Rover Series III in deep forest green rounded the bend, its restored paint gleaming in the morning sun. The vehicle looked like it had driven straight out of a storybook about the Irish countryside.

Grace's steps slowed as she recognized the driver.

Sean pulled up alongside her, one arm resting on the open window frame. "Let me guess. You're not lost. You're just photographing the local wildlife?"

"I love sheep," she said almost seriously, then followed his eyes to her muddy boots—at least, she hoped it was mud. "And I'm not lost. I'm going to the Black Church. It's right over there." She pointed to the ruins on the hill.

"About four miles away, over private land and three stream crossings." His mouth twitched. "I thought, after yesterday, you might be done with getting stranded in the middle of nowhere."

"I brought an umbrella this time."

"Very prepared." He reached across and pushed open the passenger door. "Get in. I know a better way."

Grace hesitated only briefly before climbing up into the Land Rover. The interior smelled of well-oiled leather and something distinctly mechanical but pleasant. "This is beautiful," she said, running a hand over the pristine dashboard. "I didn't expect a tech entrepreneur to drive a decades-old car."

He shot her a look, and she felt herself flush. "I, uh, might have googled you last night."

"Ah." He navigated around a bend in the narrow lane. "And here I thought I was maintaining my groundskeeper mystique so well."

"Not bad. This Land Rover fits that image better than your tech mogul one."

"It was my father's." His voice softened. "I restored it last year after I moved back. Needed something to do with my hands after spending ten years staring at screens." He glanced sideways at her. "You disappointed it's not a Ferrari?"

"Actually, I like it." She did, surprisingly, quite a lot. Like the house, it spoke of someone who valued heritage without being trapped by it. "Though I notice you waited until after I was thoroughly soaked yesterday to mention you had a car."

"Would you have gotten into a stranger's vehicle?"

"Probably not."

"Well then. But now that you—and Google—know me so well..." He turned onto a narrow track she would never have found on her own. "Consider yesterday's drenching a trust-building exercise."

Grace laughed despite herself. The Land Rover handled the rough track with ease, and Sean drove with the confidence of someone who knew every rut and hollow. They passed through a gate (which he got out to open and close, waving away her offer to help), and suddenly, the ruins loomed before them, more impressive up close.

"The thing about the Black Church," Sean said as he parked, "is that you can't really appreciate it without knowing all the local spots." He grabbed a water bottle from behind his seat. "Care for the full tour?"

Grace looked at him—at this man who could have been driving any luxury car in the world but chose to restore his father's old Land Rover. Here he was offering to spend his morning showing a stranger around when he probably had a dozen more important things to do.

"I'd like that," she said.

The morning mist clung to the ruins as they approached. Grace could have sworn the shadows lengthened as they drew near as if the old stones themselves were watching. A lone blackbird called from somewhere in the twisted hawthorn hedgerow, its song echoing strangely in the quiet.

"It's beautiful," Grace said softly, reaching out to touch the weathered stone. "Even blackened and crumbling like this."

"The stones remember." Sean's voice was quiet, his hand trailing along the wall where generations of hands had touched before. "That's what my grandmother always said. 'The stones of Ireland remember every story they've witnessed.'"

Grace thought of the storyteller at the Harbor

Light. "Your grandmother must have known so many stories about this place. About Kathleen—"

"Ah, so you've heard."

"Last night at the pub."

"Of course." He gave her a sidelong glance. "About my many-times-great grandmother and her storm-crossed love—" He paused beneath the remnants of the church window. "The story they tell at the Harbor Light is not the whole tale. My grandmother knew the true ending."

"What is it?"

"They found each other again, " he said simply.

Grace waited expectantly. "And...?"

"And what?" His mouth twitched at the corner.

"And what's the rest of the story?"

"Now, Grace, I believe I've mentioned that I'm not a storyteller, but I'll tell you my grandmother's version as close to her words as I can recall."

He looked into the distance. "Rory was bedridden for weeks, but in time, he recovered. Two decades later, her husband died, and she knew in her heart where she must go on Lughnasadh eve when the veil between what is and what might have been grows thin. That's when they'd first fallen in love, you see—at the harvest dance.

"The storm that blew in from the sea that night was fierce enough to make even the bravest soul think twice. Her stable master begged her not to go. He said no horse would carry her through such weather, and indeed, her mare reared and fought the bridle until Kathleen knew she'd have to make her way on foot.

"The path to the church was treacherous enough in daylight. In the storm's darkness, with the wind trying to sweep her off the cliff's edge and the rain stinging like needles, every step was an act of faith. They say she fell more times than she could count, crawling sometimes on her hands and knees when the wind was too strong to stand. Her fine dress was in tatters, but still, she pressed on.

"When lightning split the sky, she could see the church ahead, black against the clouds. There she was, on the same path where Rory had fallen all those years ago. Perhaps it was madness that drove her forward, or perhaps it was love—though some say they are one and the same.

"And there, in the doorway of the church, stood Rory. As if he'd known she would come. As if he'd been waiting all those years for that storm, for that night, and that moment."

A cool breeze stirred Grace's hair, carrying the scent of wild roses and distant rain. "How did he know she'd come?"

"The old ones say it was their love that conjured the storm to draw them back together." Sean's eyes met hers, green as the hills after rain. "Or perhaps they were just sentimental about Lughnasadh, the day they'd first found love. But my grandmother said it was love—simple as that."

"That's..." Grace swallowed, struck by the quiet

intensity in his face. She couldn't help thinking of Olivia's insistence on a Lughnasadh wedding and how Grace had dismissed it as a silly superstition. "That's quite a story."

"The barkeep prefers the tragic ending." His usual reserve started to return, but his hand lingered on the stone as if reluctant to break the connection. "Better for business at the pub. Sparks more conversation and drink orders." He grinned.

A shaft of sunlight broke through the clouds, catching the blackened walls and making them gleam like wet ink. For just a moment, Grace could have sworn she saw the church as it once must have been— white stone glowing in candlelight, a beacon of hope in a storm.

"The festival's coming up soon," Grace said, recalling the canceled wedding plans.

"Next week." He gave her another of those sidelong glances that made her heart skip. "Though I suppose you won't be here for that."

Grace thought of her return ticket, which she'd already rescheduled for three days before the festival. "No, I suppose not."

The blackbird called again. Its song was almost like laughter on the morning air.

LATER THAT NIGHT, Grace sat at the small desk in her room, her laptop open to her work calendar. She should have been checking on her other clients' weddings but instead found herself opening her journal app and typing *July 29th - Black Church ruins with Sean.*

She stared at the date, three days before what would have been Olivia's mystically perfect wedding. *I hadn't expected to find anything magical here, let alone...* She deleted the note without finishing the thought.

But she found herself remembering the way Sean's hand had traced the church's weathered stones and the quiet reverence in his voice as he'd told the rest of Kathleen and Rory's story. For someone who claimed not to be a storyteller, he'd made her feel the power of a love that survived time and circumstance.

"Don't be ridiculous," she told herself firmly, closing the laptop. She was a wedding planner who'd just had her latest project implode because of a fortune-teller. The last thing she needed was to start believing in old Irish legends about perfect dates and destined loves. But as she got ready for bed, she couldn't help glancing at her phone one more time, making sure the date was safely stored in her calendar.

SEAN STOOD in his glass-walled study, watching the sun rise over the sea. The previous day with Grace had left him unsettled in a way he hadn't felt since leaving Dublin.

He'd fled the tech world's constant networking, the endless social obligations, and the expectation to be "on" every moment. Here at Clonmara, he'd been content with the simplicity of familiar stone walls, ancient traditions, and the company of people he'd known all his life. In short, he'd found peace.

Until Grace.

He moved to the cabinet where he kept the family albums and pulled out the oldest one. The leather binding was cracked at the edges, and dark century-old paper crumbled at the edges as he carefully opened it. Inside was a drawing of Kathleen— his many-times-great grandmother, her eyes hauntingly similar to Grace's. The same mix of practicality and hidden romance—of skepticism and hope.

His grandmother used to say the Callahan men were cursed—or blessed, depending on how you looked at it—to fall for women who challenged everything they thought they knew about themselves.

Grace's camera case had slipped from her shoulder when she'd leaned in to study the church ruins' weathered carvings. He'd caught it before it fell, their hands brushing. She'd thanked him with that smile that managed to be both professional and piercing—that smile that made him want to...

He abruptly set down the album. This was madness. She lived in Boston and ran a successful business that was all about people, celebrations, and constant social interaction. Everything he'd fled Dublin to escape. He could barely tolerate the tech investors' dinner parties—what could he possibly offer a woman who orchestrated joy for a living?

But he couldn't stop thinking about the way she'd listened to his grandmother's version of the legend, how her initial skepticism had softened into something like wonder, and, most of all, how she'd asked about the festival with poorly hidden longing in her voice.

Through the window, he could see storm clouds gathering. There would be rain tomorrow, maybe even through the weekend. His hand hovered over his phone. He didn't have her number, but he knew where she was staying. The day before, he'd dropped her off at O'Brien's. But the thought of calling the B&B made his stomach twist. Mrs. O'Brien's knowing tone and the inevitable audience of curious locals who might overhear made him cringe.

The sensible thing would be to let Grace go back to America and her world of weddings, leaving him to the quiet life he'd carved out for himself.

Before he could think better of it, he picked up the phone.

"O'Brien's Bed and Breakfast," came the landlady's cheerful voice.

"Mrs. O'Brien, it's Sean Callahan. I was wondering if... That is... Could you..." He closed his eyes. "Is Grace Luong available?"

"Sean! It's lovely to hear from you. Just a

moment." He could hear the smile in her voice and picture the heads turning in the parlor as Mrs. O'Brien practically sang, "Grace, dear! Phone for you —it's young Mr. Callahan from Clonmara House!"

He heard a flurry of muffled conversation in the background and then a sudden silence.

Grace's voice came next, warm but uncertain. "Hello?"

"Grace? I was wondering..." He turned to watch the storm clouds gathering. "Are you busy this evening?"

THE SECRET GARDEN at Clonmara House was a world unto itself, tucked behind high stone walls draped with climbing roses. Golden evening light slanted through old apple trees, catching the mist from a trickling fountain. At a small wrought-iron table, its scrollwork painted white and weathered by countless Irish summers, Sean had set out a simple dinner.

"My mother created this space," he said, pouring wine into delicate glasses. "She said every house needs a secret garden."

Grace settled into one of the matching chairs, running her fingers over the intricate metalwork. "Your mother was right. It's beautiful. So peaceful."

"That's why I came back home." Sean sat across from her, the small table making the moment feel intimate. "After Dublin, after the tech world...I missed this place."

"Was it that bad?"

He studied his wine glass. "Have you ever felt when you're planning one of your weddings that everyone's so focused on the production that they've forgotten what matters?"

Grace nodded, surprised by his insight.

"Dublin was like that. Constant networking, people always wanting something. Even dating became tactical—every relationship analyzed for strategic advantage." He gave a self-deprecating smile. "The last woman I dated had her assistant research my net worth before our first dinner."

"That's horrible."

"It was clarifying. Made me realize how far I'd drifted from anything real." He looked up, meeting her eyes. "What about you? Do you ever get tired of orchestrating other people's happiness?"

The question caught her off guard with its perception. In the gentle evening light, with the garden's perfume surrounding them, Grace's guard slipped.

"Sometimes, I wonder if I chose this career because it was safer to manage other people's love stories than risk having my own." She traced the rim of her wine glass. "My parents had this amazing marriage—the kind where they still looked at each other like newlyweds after twenty years. When Dad died, Mom never even looked at another man. That kind of love... It's scary. Amazing, but scary."

They sat in silence for a moment as the garden grew darker around them. It wasn't an uncomfortable silence—more like the pause between movements in a chamber music suite.

His eyes twinkled. "So, all those elaborate weddings and couples in love must be really scary." He smiled, but Grace remained serious.

"Actually, I don't really see that kind of love as much as you'd think. To be honest, after planning so many elaborate weddings, I think Kathleen and Rory did it best. Two people alone in a chapel. What more do you need, really? But each other?"

Sean went very still. When she looked up, the intensity in his eyes made her breath catch.

"Dance with me?" he asked suddenly.

"Here?"

He pulled out his phone, and soft music filled their secluded paradise. He held out his hand, and his eyes fixed hers. "Here."

Dancing in the garden felt different from any dance Grace had ever known. Sean drew her close, one hand warm against her back, the other still holding hers over his heart. The roses released their evening perfume, mixing with the herb garden's earthier scents. Above them, the first stars appeared.

"Grace." His voice was rough.

When she looked up, the tenderness in his face made her heart stumble. He traced her cheek with his free hand, giving her time to pull away if she wanted to. But she didn't want to. She lifted her face to his, and when their lips met, it was like coming home.

The kiss deepened slowly as if they had all the time in the world. His hands cradled her face while hers gripped his shoulders, anchoring herself as everything else fell away. He tasted of wine and something essentially him, and he kissed like a man who'd been holding himself back for far too long.

When they finally broke apart, the stars were fully out, creating a canopy of light above their secret garden. Sean rested his forehead against hers, his thumbs stroking her cheeks.

"Stay," he whispered. "For the festival."

Grace's heart twisted. "My flight's on Tuesday. I have to be back in Boston by..."

"Change it." His voice was soft but certain. "Stay longer."

She thought of Kathleen and Rory, of chances lost and found. "I want to. I really do."

He kissed her again, slower this time, deeper, as if trying to convince her without words. Above them, clouds were gathering over the sea, promising rain.

THE DRIVE back to the B&B was quiet, filled with shared glances and unspoken words. Sean pulled the Land Rover to a stop and came around to open her door. As they reached the front steps, Grace noticed a slight movement at the parlor window curtain.

"I don't think we're exactly alone," she murmured, nodding toward where the lace curtain had definitely twitched.

"Mrs. O'Brien does seem invested in the evening's outcome." Sean's eyes gleamed with unexpected mischief. Then, before Grace could respond, he pulled her into his arms and kissed her. This wasn't the gentle exploration of their garden kisses— this was a kiss that made her knees weak and her heart race, a kiss that said everything they hadn't yet put into words.

When he finally released her, Grace had to grip the porch railing to steady herself.

"Goodnight, Grace," he said softly, and she could have sworn there was a hint of satisfaction in his voice at her obvious dizziness.

She managed to make it inside, where Mrs. O'Brien was suddenly very busy arranging flowers that had already been perfectly arranged.

"Lovely evening," the innkeeper said innocently.

"Yes, it is." Grace hoped the darkness had hidden her blush. "Goodnight, Mrs. O'Brien."

She fled up the stairs and practically floated into her room. The whole evening had been impossibly perfect. Sean was like no one she'd ever known, let alone dated. But how could she even call it dating when she was going back home in a couple of days?

Whatever it was, he could kiss! She could still feel his lips—tender yet passionate enough to curl her toes.

She paused and thought about staying longer—through Lughnasadh. It was just a few days, and she hadn't told Megan she was coming home early. She stared at her phone, then pulled up her airline's website. One click and she could have the rest of the week here with Sean and his heart-soaring kisses.

As her finger hovered over the Modify Booking button, her heart raced with possibility.

Her phone rang, and Megan's name lit up the screen.

"Grace? Thank God. We have a situation with the Turner wedding."

No! This is not happening! She winced. "What kind of situation?"

"The venue just flooded—burst pipe. The wedding's in three days, and they're talking about suing if we can't find something comparable."

Reality landed on her like a bucket of cold water. This was her biggest wedding of the year—in the works for eighteen months.

"I need you back here, Grace. Tonight, if possible."

She looked out her window. It was too dark to see, but somewhere out there, Sean was on his way back to Clonmara House. She wished she'd gone with him.

"I'll..." Her throat felt tight. "I'll book the first flight I can get."

Two DAYS LATER, Grace hung up the phone, leaned back in her office chair, and finally allowed herself to breathe. The new venue was secured. The Turner wedding was saved, even if a hundred details still needed adjusting.

But her heart was in Ireland.

SHE CLOSED her eyes and remembered the frantic packing in the pre-dawn darkness. When, well after midnight, she'd left Sean a goodbye text, he immediately called back and insisted on driving her to the Dublin Airport. The hour didn't matter. It was settled.

The Land Rover's headlights had cut through the night as they wound their way along the coast road. They'd barely spoken, both knowing that words would only make it harder.

Can't we just go back to the Black Church? she'd blurted out.

I'd take you there in a heartbeat. His voice had been rough with emotion.

But when they reached the airport departures entrance, reality set in. One last kiss, one embrace, and she forced herself to walk away.

Now, two days later, she couldn't stop thinking about him, about dances in secret gardens, and the way he looked at her as though nothing else mattered.

Her computer dinged with another email about the Turner wedding. Megan had already handled half the vendor calls and coordinated the new floor plan.

Grace sat up straight. Maybe...

She found Megan in the conference room, surrounded by seating charts.

"The Turners are happy with the new venue?" Grace asked.

"Ecstatic. Mrs. Turner says it's even better than the original."

"That's great! So...could you maybe...handle the rest of it?"

Megan looked up, a slow smile spreading across her face. "You want to go back to Ireland."

Grace shook her head. "No, it's too much to ask."

"Are you kidding? Grace, in five years, I've watched you make everyone else's love stories come true. Maybe it's time for yours." Megan's eyes sparkled. "Go. I've got this. The Turners love me, the vendors are all confirmed, and you've trained me for exactly this moment."

"But—"

"You're in love! For once in your life, be the bride instead of the planner." Megan was already reaching for her phone. "I'm booking your flight right now. When's this festival thing?"

"Lughnasadh. It's tomorrow."

"Perfect. If you leave tonight, you'll make it." Megan's fingers flew over her keyboard while her phone was on hold. "Oh, look! You've got miles! Guess who's flying business? Shh, don't argue! You'll need to sleep on the plane." She looked up, phone in hand. "Go home and pack. I'll email your ticket."

Five hours later, Grace sat on a plane, glass of Champagne in hand, her heart racing. She was really doing this—following her heart instead of her carefully planned schedule.

Kathleen had braved a wild storm for true love. Aer Lingus wasn't exactly a storm, but if this wasn't true love... But it was.

SEAN COULD HEAR the festival starting up in the village as distant music and laughter drifted on the wind. He should be there. Mrs. Flynn had reminded him twice already that the whole village would expect him to make an appearance—and he would. His wolfhound, Finn, had done his best to interfere with his plans, eagerly following Sean to the car. Maybe it was better this way. At least he'd have Finn's company.

He found himself driving the familiar coastal road, the Land Rover knowing the way almost without his guidance. The Black Church ruins appeared against the darkening sky, and he pulled over.

He'd been avoiding the place since Grace left. But today, with the festival in full swing and memories of their conversation in the garden haunting him, he needed... What? Solitude? Connection?

Two people alone in a chapel, she'd said that night, her eyes soft in the garden's twilight. *What more do you need, really? But each other?*

The words had lodged in his heart, a truth so simple it hurt. After years of tech launches and investor meetings, of trying to be what everyone expected of Sean Callahan, a successful entrepreneur, she'd seen right through to what he really wanted. Just two people, being real with each other.

Storm clouds were gathering over the sea as he approached the ruins. A few drops of rain struck his face, and he remembered Grace's voice. *Kathleen and Rory did it best.*

He touched the weathered stone, remembering how she'd done the same. A professional wedding planner who believed the simplest ceremony was the most meaningful. The irony might have made him smile if he wasn't aching with missing her.

Thunder rolled in the distance as if signaling him to head to the festival. He called Finn, who had gone off exploring. The festival would be moving indoors soon to shelter from the approaching storm. But something kept him there, watching the clouds coming in from the west.

"JUST PULL OVER HERE," Grace said as the Black Church ruins came into view through the misty rain.

"You're sure about this?" Tommy glanced at the gathering storm clouds. "Festival's starting in the village. It'll be much drier there."

"I know. I just need a few minutes."

The taxi rounded the last bend, and Grace's heart nearly stopped. There, parked at the edge of the path, was a familiar forest-green Land Rover.

"Well, now," Tommy said softly, "isn't that interesting?"

Grace's words came out in a whisper, "On second thought, just leave me here."

Her hands trembled as she paid the fare.

When Tommy helped her with her suitcase, his eyes were kind. "Some things," he said, "are worth getting a bit wet for."

As the taxi's taillights disappeared into the growing darkness. The wind tugged at her hair, carrying the scent of rain and sea salt. Somewhere in those ruins was Sean. He'd come here too, drawn by the same pull she'd felt halfway across an ocean.

Taking a deep breath, Grace dragged her suitcase up the path toward the church. On the way, Finn bounded up to her, and she laughed as she scratched behind his ears. His tail wagged with such enthu-siasm his whole body swayed.

Thunder rolled overhead, but for once in her life, she didn't care about the storm. She reached the top of the hill, rounded the corner, and there he was. His tall frame filled the ancient doorway.

For a moment, neither of them moved. The rain fell harder, but Grace barely noticed. Sean's eyes held hers across the space between them, and in those green eyes, she saw everything she'd flown across an ocean to find.

Two people alone in a chapel.

What more did anyone need, really?

THANK YOU!

Thank you for reading! If you enjoyed this book, please consider leaving a review or a rating. Your feedback on bookstore, Goodreads, and Bookbub websites helps other readers discover books they'll enjoy.

instagram.com/jljarvis.writer

facebook.com/jljarvis1writer

x.com/JLJarvis_writer

youtube.com/@jljarvis-author

goodreads.com/jljarvis

bookbub.com/authors/j-l-jarvis

ALSO BY J.L. JARVIS

Waterfront Summers

(Can be read in any order)

The Cottage at Peregrine Cove

The House on Serenity Lake

Moonlight on Mariner's Bluff

Drake & Wilde Mysteries

(Reading Order)

Love in the Time of Pumpkins

Secrets in the Hollow

Shadow of the Horseman

Standalones

(Can be read in any order)

A Cowboy Kind of Love

A Christmas Eve Stop

Christmas by Lamplight

A Kiss in the Rain

App-ily Ever After

Once Upon a Winter

The Red Rose

Highland Vow

Short Stories

(Can be read in any order)

The Magic of Snow

The Eleventh-Hour Pact

A Christmas Yarn

The Farmer and the Belle

Work-Crush Balance

Cedar Creek

(Can be read in any order)

Christmas at Cedar Creek

Snowstorm at Cedar Creek

Sunlight on Cedar Creek

Pine Harbor

(Reading Order)

Allison's Pine Harbor Summer

Evelyn's Pine Harbor Autumn

Lydia's Pine Harbor Christmas

Holiday House

(Can be read in any order)

The Christmas Cabin

The Winter Lodge

The Lighthouse

The Christmas Castle

The Beach House

The Christmas Tree Inn

The Holiday Hideaway

Highland Passage

(Can be read in any order)

Highland Passage

Knight Errant

Lost Bride

Highland Soldiers

(Reading Order)

The Enemy

The Betrayal

The Return

The Wanderer

American Hearts

(Can be read in any order)

Secret Hearts

Forbidden Hearts

Runaway Hearts

For more information, visit jljarvis.com.

Get monthly book news at news.jljarvis.com.

ABOUT THE AUTHOR

J.L. Jarvis is a left-handed former opera singer/teacher/lawyer who writes books. She now lives and writes on a mountaintop in upstate New York.

jljarvis.com